Common Core Lessons & Activities:
Water Cycle

By Carole Marsh
Published by Gallopade International, Inc.

Printed in the U.S.A. (Peachtree City, Georgia)

TABLE OF CONTENTS

G: Includes Graphic Organizer
GO: Graphic Organizer is also available 8½" x 11" online
download at www.gallopade.com/client/go
(numbers above correspond to the graphic organizer numbers online)

READING INFORMATIONAL TEXT

Water on Earth

Read the text and answer the questions.

It may seem like the Earth has an unlimited supply of water, but the supply of water is actually limited. Water on Earth is not gained or lost—it just goes around and around in what we call the "water cycle." The water cycle is the movement of water from the ground to the air and back to the ground in a continuous pattern. Amazingly, the water on Earth today has been on Earth since the time of the dinosaurs, and a long time before that!

The water cycle moves Earth's water to many places and in many forms. Most of Earth's water is found in the oceans. Water can be found frozen in glaciers, too. Water is in the air we breathe and the food we eat. Water floats above our heads as clouds and falls to the Earth as rain, sleet, and snow. Water calmly rests in lakes and reservoirs. It ripples through streams and plummets down waterfalls. Water seeps into the Earth and flows underground.

The movement of water through the water cycle brings life-giving water to all living things. All plants and animals need water in order to survive. In fact, water is a key ingredient of all plants and animals. Did you know 60% of the human body is made of water? Without the water cycle, life on Earth would not exist. Water is essential for all of Earth's living things.

1. Use the text to define limited, then give a synonym and antonym.
2. **True** or **False**: The water cycle creates new water.
3. A. Use the text to define water cycle.
   B. Why is this process described as a "cycle"?
4. List at least five verbs from the text that describe the movement of water through the water cycle.
5. Match the following questions to whether they are best answered by paragraph 1, 2, or 3 of the text.
   A. _____ Why is water important?
   B. _____ What is the water cycle?
   C. _____ Where is water on Earth?
6. Describe the relationship between the water cycle and life on Earth.

READING INFORMATIONAL TEXT

Water, Water, Everywhere

Read the texts and answer the questions.

Dictionary entry: <u>scarce</u>: (adjective) rare, uncommon, in short supply

Water covers about 70% of the Earth's surface. However, approximately 97% of ALL the Earth's water is "saltwater" found in the oceans. Saltwater is not safe for humans to drink. Only about 3% of all water is "freshwater." Approximately ¾ of all freshwater is frozen in polar ice caps and glaciers. The remaining ¼ of freshwater, which is what we use for drinking, cleaning, and growing crops, is found in lakes, rivers, and underground.

1. *"Plentiful" is an antonym (opposite) of "scarce".*
   A. Use the dictionary entry for "scarce" to define "plentiful".
   B. What type of water is plentiful on Earth?
   C. What type of water is scarce on Earth?

2. Make inferences from the text to determine whether each statement is **true** or **false**. Correct any false statement to be true.
   A. ______ Most of Earth's saltwater is frozen.
   B. ______ 97% of Earth's water is drinkable.
   C. ______ About 30% of the Earth's surface is NOT covered by water.

3. To complete each chart, use colored pencils to shade in the chart based on data in the text, add a key to explain what each color means, and write the percentages for each area shaded.
   A. Use Chart 1 to show what percentage of Earth's water is saltwater and what percentage is freshwater.
   B. Use Chart 2 to show Earth's freshwater divided into 2 categories: "ice caps and glaciers" and "freshwater available for human use."

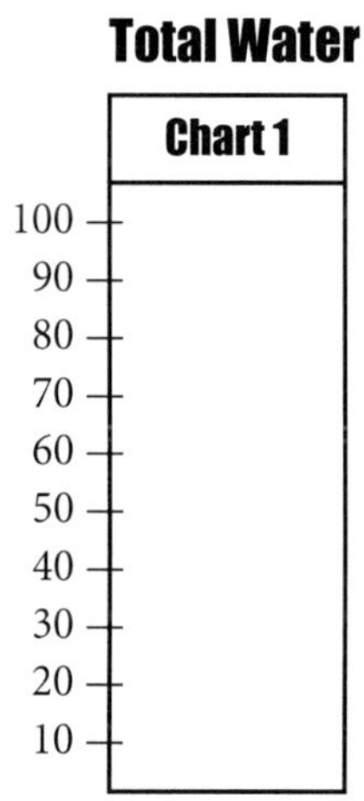

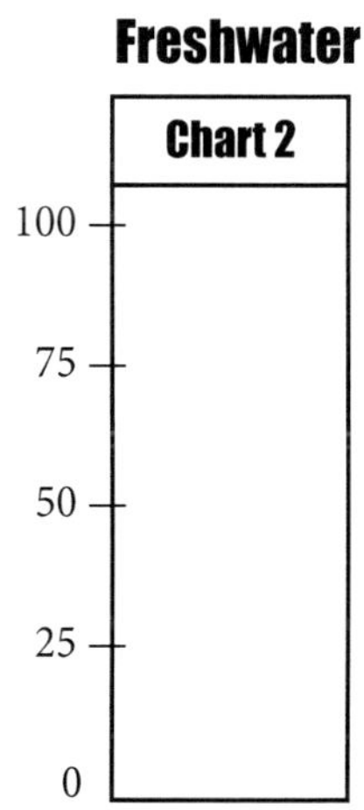

A Simple Water Cycle

Read the text and answer the questions.

1) Evaporation: When water on the Earth's surface (such as in lakes and the ocean) is warmed by the sun, it changes into a gas (water vapor) and rises into the air.

2) Condensation: When water vapor rises into the air, it cools and changes into a liquid, forming tiny water droplets that clump together and become visible as clouds. When condensation happens near the ground, it creates fog or dew.

3) Precipitation: When water droplets in the clouds become too heavy, they fall back to Earth; depending on temperature, the water that falls can be liquid (rain) or solid (snow, sleet, or hail).

4) Accumulation: After precipitation falls to the Earth, it runs across the ground or seeps into the ground, and travels until it joins a body of water. Water accumulates, or collects, in lakes, rivers, the ocean, and pockets underground.

1. Use the text to label each process on the water cycle diagram:
   A. evaporation B. condensation C. precipitation D. accumulation

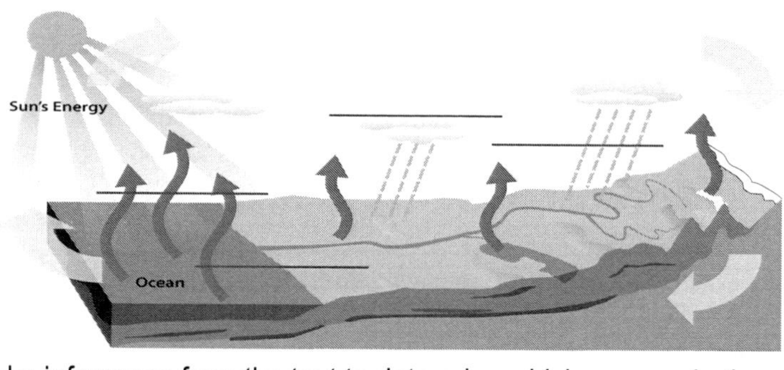

2. Make inferences from the text to determine which process in the water cycle is most directly a cause of:
   A. ______ clouds
   B. ______ flooding
   C. ______ humidity (moisture in the air)
   D. ______ snow

3. Use the text and what you know about weather to describe the relationship between the water cycle and weather.

The Sun

Read the text and answer the questions.

Heat from the sun is an essential part of the water cycle. Without heat from the sun, all of the Earth's water would be frozen, and there would be no water cycle! Additionally, the sun is the driving force of the water cycle—it gets everything moving.

As the sun warms the Earth, it causes some of the water in the oceans to evaporate. Clouds form as the evaporated water condensates high up in the sky. As the sun warms the Earth, it also increases the temperature of land and water. However, it increases the temperatures unevenly, because land heats and cools more quickly than water does. The difference in temperatures causes air over land and water to move, creating wind. The large land and water areas of continents and oceans create wind patterns. Wind patterns are also created and affected by the Earth's rotation. As a result of wind patterns, much of the water that evaporates from the ocean ends up as clouds over land!

1. Number the steps in the order they occur:
   A. ______ clouds form
   B. ______ some water evaporates
   C. ______ sun warms water on the Earth
   D. ______ water vapor condensates
2. Explain how the sun causes wind.
3. A. Why is wind important to the water cycle?
   B. How is the Earth's rotation important to the water cycle?
   C. How would the water cycle change if there was no wind or rotation of the Earth?
   D. How would this affect you?
4. Use the text to complete the graphic organizer.

How the Sun Affects the Water Cycle

Evaporation & Transpiration

Read the text and answer the questions.

Evaporation occurs when water is heated and changes to a gas (water vapor). In the water cycle, this occurs when the sun shines on bodies of water, such as oceans, lakes, rivers, and ponds. The sun causes the water to heat up and some of it turns into water vapor in the air. About 90% of all water vapor in the air is a result of evaporation.

Plants produce water vapor too. Plants gather water and nutrients from the soil through their roots. They use this to produce food and energy. Plants return some of the water back to the air. They release water, in the form of water vapor, through tiny pores on the surface of their leaves. This process is called transpiration. A large oak tree can produce 40,000 gallons of water vapor every year through transpiration. About 10% of all water vapor in the air is a result of transpiration from plants.

Evaporation and transpiration are the two parts of the water cycle that return the water on Earth back to the atmosphere.

1. Define evaporation and transpiration as they are used in the text.
2. Predict what would happen if evaporation and transpiration did not occur. Cite evidence from the text to support your answer.
3. Use the Venn diagram to compare and contrast evaporation and transpiration.

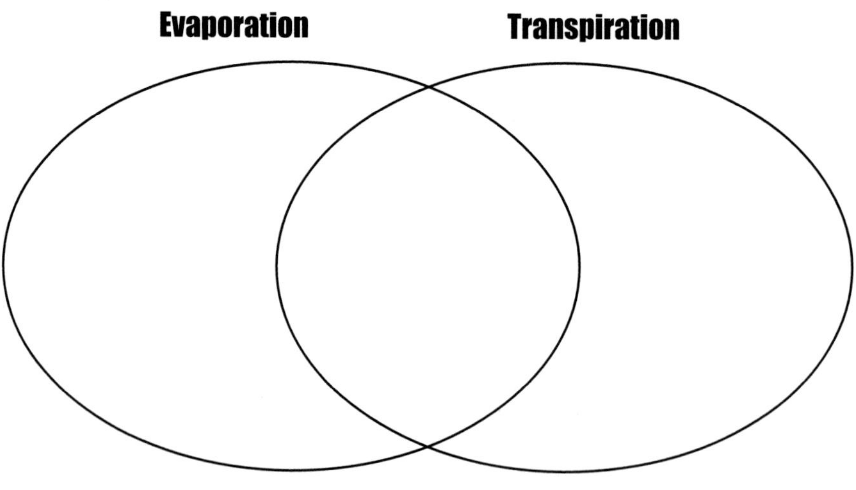

Condensation

Read the text and answer the questions.

1) Condensation is the process by which water vapor in the air cools and changes from gas to liquid. Condensation can be seen or felt in a variety of different ways. One of these ways—when you see clouds form in the sky—is an essential part of the water cycle!

2) Have you ever had a really cold drink outside on a hot, humid day? You may have seen and felt condensation! The cold temperature of a glass (or can or bottle) causes water vapor in the air near the glass to cool. When it does, the water clumps into tiny droplets that form on the outside of the cold glass. Similarly, if you wear glasses, you might have noticed your glasses fog up when going from a cool room to the hot outside—that is condensation!

3) Have you ever walked outside in the morning and noticed the ground was wet, but it did not rain during the night? You saw and felt condensation! Typically, the air temperature cools at nighttime. If there is too much water vapor in the air for the cool air to hold, the excess water is released from the air as it turns from gas to liquid. The water forms droplets on the ground, called dew.

4) You see condensation when you look up into the sky and see clouds. High up in the sky, cool air temperatures cause the water vapor in the air to change from gas to liquid, forming tiny water droplets. When there are many of these small droplets together, they form clouds. Wind causes clouds to move, so the water that eventually gets released often helps deliver fresh water to dry land.

1. A. Explain how water changes during condensation.
   B. Explain how air changes during condensation.
2. Illustrate the four examples of condensation described in the text. In each illustration, draw and label what happens to the water vapor in the air.
3. A. What do you think was the author's purpose of this text?
   B. Describe the organizational structure the author used.
   C. Who does the text refer to when the word "you" is used?
   D. In your opinion, was the author successful? Why or why not?

Forms of Precipitation

Read the text and answer the questions.

Precipitation is water that falls from a cloud to the Earth's surface. Precipitation is often rain, but it is not always rain. Air temperature influences what form of precipitation occurs.

When air temperatures are above freezing, precipitation usually falls as rain. Sometimes, the air temperature up high is warm enough for water droplets to fall from clouds as rain, but the air temperature near the ground is below freezing. The rain gets super cold as it passes through this cold air, and then it freezes on impact when it hits the ground. This is called freezing rain.

When air temperatures are below freezing, water droplets in the clouds freeze, stick together, and fall as snow. Sometimes snow falls through a layer of warm air on the way to the ground. This warm air melts some of the snow, but then it freezes again as it passes through cold air near the ground. When this happens, the precipitation is called sleet, instead of snow.

Hail is a form of precipitation that often occurs during thunderstorms. Air in the storm gets below freezing and ice crystals form. Strong winds in the thunderstorm prevent the ice crystals from falling all the way to the ground. Instead, new layers of ice form around the ice crystals, causing them to get bigger and bigger. Eventually, the hailstones become so big and heavy they fall to the ground. Hailstones can be as large as a golf ball or even a baseball!

1. Use the text to define precipitation.
2. What is the relationship between air temperature and precipitation?
3. A. Create simple diagrams for the 5 forms of precipitation described in the text. In each diagram, show how the precipitation is formed, and the process that occurs as the precipitation falls, including any stages or changes it goes through. Indicate air temperature(s) in each diagram. Add a title to each diagram to indicate what form of precipitation it illustrates.
   B. Illustrate each of the 5 forms of precipitation described in the text by drawing a scene that includes a person and his or her likely reaction or behavior in response to the type of precipitation shown.

Accumulation

Read the text and complete the graphic organizer.

Water on Earth collects in lakes, rivers, the ocean, and pockets underground. How water gets to these places varies. This process is called accumulation, and it is part of the water cycle.

When precipitation falls on land, what happens next? Sometimes it falls into a body of water, returning directly to an ocean, lake, or river. Sometimes it falls on land. When precipitation falls on land, it doesn't just stay where it fell. Sometimes the water flows across the ground until it eventually finds a body of water to join. This water is called runoff. Sometimes the water seeps into the ground, either staying in the soil or collecting in rock crevices underground. This water is called groundwater.

Runoff is responsible for refilling lakes and rivers that have evaporated or been used by humans. Many cities and communities use the water in lakes and rivers for drinking, cooking, and cleaning. Runoff in streams and lakes provides water for nearby plants and animal wildlife as well.

Groundwater is found as moisture in the soil and it collects in deep underground pools. Trees and other plants absorb groundwater through their roots. People in communities dig deep wells to access groundwater for drinking, cooking, and cleaning.

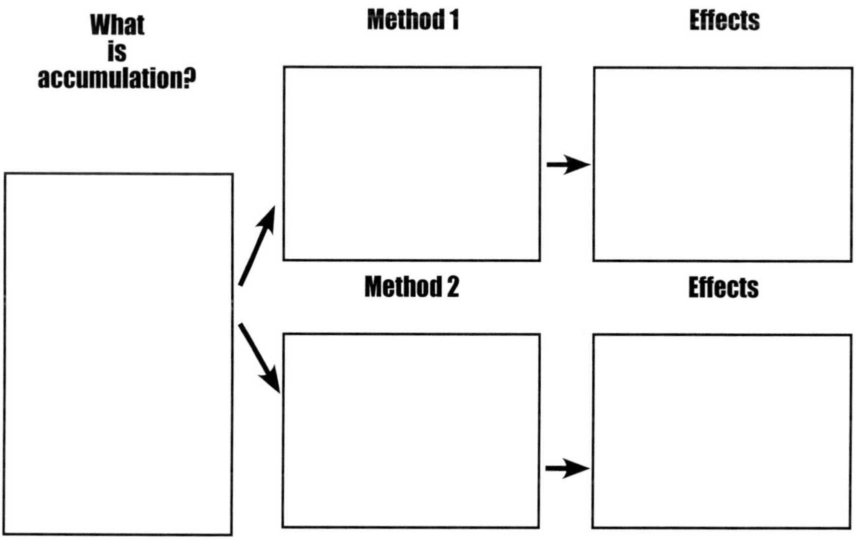

Cycle of a Cloud

Look at the tables and charts, and answer the questions.

Condensation:		
Water vapor rises up to where air gets cool.	Cool air causes the water vapor to turn into tiny water droplets.	

Evaporation:		
Sun warms the water in lakes and oceans.	Water (liquid) turns into water vapor (gas).	

Precipitation:		
Water droplets get too heavy to stay in the atmosphere.	Water droplets clump together and get bigger.	

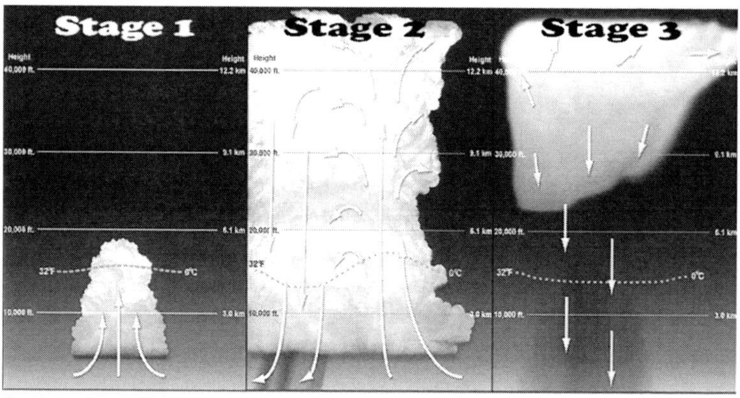

Courtesy of the NOAA

1. Complete the three tables by adding the ending steps below:
   A. Tiny water droplets gather and form clouds.
   B. Water falls to the earth.
   C. Water vapor rises in the atmosphere.
2. What do the arrows in the diagram indicate?
3. Indicate which stage of the diagram shows each process below:
   A. ___ Precipitation B. ___ Evaporation C. _____ Condensation
4. A. What causes the movement of water in Stage 1?
   B. What causes the movement of water in Stage 2?
   C. What causes the movement of water in Stage 3?

EXPERIMENT

A Model of the Water Cycle

Read the text and answer the questions.

My Science Fair Project: A Water Cycle Model

First, I poured several cups of water, into a large metal bowl. Next, I placed an empty mug, bottom-down, in the water. Then, I placed a sheet of plastic wrap over the top of the bowl, and I secured it with a rubber band.

My model had all the important parts of the water cycle, except for one. I needed a source of heat! Very carefully, I moved the bowl next to the window where the sun was shining in. As the sun warmed my model, I watched and took notes.

After five minutes, I saw small water droplets form on the underside of the plastic wrap. I also noticed the water level in the bottom of the bowl had decreased. As I continued to watch, more and more water droplets formed on the plastic wrap. Then, some of the water droplets drip from the plastic wrap, down into the bowl. As the droplets fell, some water collected in the bottom of the mug.

1. Use the text to create a list of all materials that you would need to re-create this science fair project.

2. Identify which parts of the model represent these parts of the water cycle:
   A. _____ Earth
   B. _____ Ocean
   C. _____ Land
   D. _____ Atmosphere
   E. _____ Sun

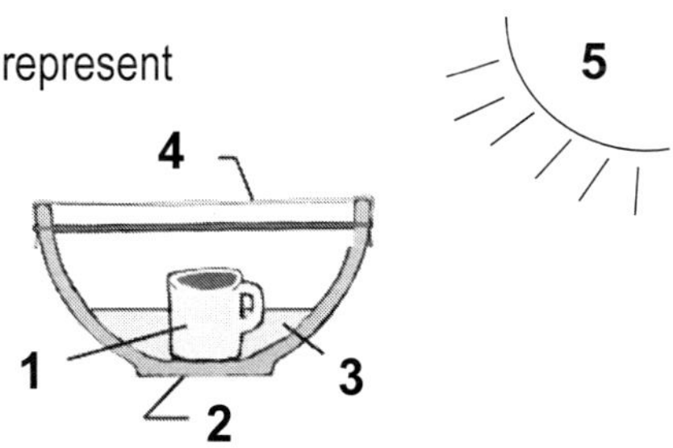

3. Identify which step of the water cycle (evaporation, condensation, precipitation, or accumulation) is represented by each of these observations from the text:
   A. _____ “water droplets formed on the plastic wrap”
   B. _____ “some water collected in the bottom of the mug”
   C. _____ “water level in the bottom of the bowl had decreased”
   D. _____ “water droplets dripped from the plastic wrap”

GRAPHIC ORGANIZER

The Water Cycle

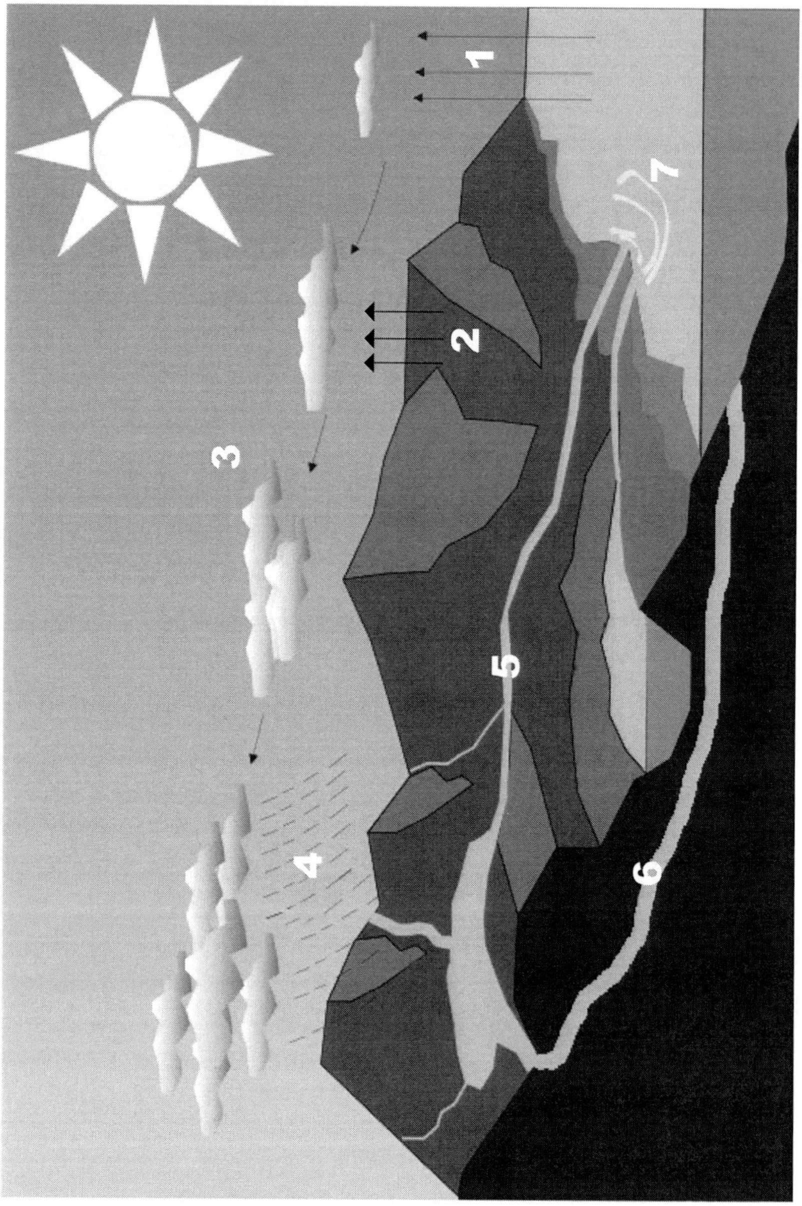

Courtesy of Wikimedia Commons

Number each statement to match the water cycle process it describes:

_____ Water from rain or melted snow and ice soaks into soil and through loose rocks into underground pools where it stays until it is used or continues to lakes or the ocean.

_____ Water vapor released by plants, rises into the atmosphere.

_____ Water in lakes and oceans turns into water vapor as the sun warms it, and the water vapor rises into the atmosphere.

_____ Water collects in a lake, ocean, or other body of water.

_____ Water falls from clouds as either a liquid or a solid.

_____ Water from rain or melted snow and ice travels across land until it becomes part of a river, lake, or ocean.

_____ Water vapor in the atmosphere cools and turns into tiny water droplets that form clouds.

Number each term to match where it occurs in the water cycle process:

_____ Accumulation

_____ Condensation

_____ Evaporation

_____ Groundwater

_____ Precipitation

_____ Runoff

_____ Transpiration

COMPARISON OF SOURCES

Rain

Read both texts and answer the questions.

Rain is a form of precipitation. Water vapor from the Earth collects as clouds until the clouds cannot hold any more moisture. The water droplets in the clouds become so heavy that they fall back to Earth as precipitation. If the temperature is above freezing, which is 32 degrees Fahrenheit or 0 degrees Celsius, the precipitation will be rain.

Rain is very important to life on Earth. Rain replaces water that has evaporated or been used from oceans, lakes, rivers, and underground wells. Rain provides people with water to drink, bathe in, and grow crops. If rain stopped falling, Earth would eventually become dry and humans could not survive.

Rainfall, the amount of rain that falls in an area, varies from place to place and is an important factor in determining what things live in an area and how they survive. Rainforests sometimes get hundreds of inches of rainfall each year. Rainforests are home to many species of life. On the other hand, deserts get very little rainfall. Few plants and animals live in deserts, and those that do often have adaptations that help them live with very little water.

The Rainy Day by Henry Wadsworth Longfellow

The day is cold, and dark, and dreary
It rains, and the wind is never weary;
The vine still clings to the mouldering wall,
But at every gust the dead leaves fall,
And the day is dark and dreary.

My life is cold, and dark, and dreary;
It rains, and the wind is never weary;
My thoughts still cling to the mouldering Past,
But the hopes of youth fall thick in the blast,
And the days are dark and dreary.

Be still, sad heart! and cease repining;
Behind the clouds is the sun still shining;
Thy fate is the common fate of all,
Into each life some rain must fall,
Some days must be dark and dreary

VOCABULARY

mouldering: (adj.) slowly falling apart

cease: (verb) come to an end

repining: (verb) feeling sad

PART A: Use the first text to answer the following questions.

1. Match the following questions to whether they are best answered by paragraph 1, 2, or 3 of the text:
   A. _____ Why is rain important?
   B. _____ Why does it rain?
   C. _____ How does rainfall affect living things?
2. Use the text to explain the difference between rain and rainfall.
3. A. List at least two ways rainfall affects rainforest areas.
   B. List at least two ways rainfall affects desert areas.

PART B: Use the second text to answer the following questions.

4. A. What is the tone of the second text?
   B. What words and phrases does the author use to create the tone?
5. What is the main message of the third stanza? Cite text from the poem to support your answer.

PART C: Compare and contrast the two texts.

6. Describe how each text characterizes rain differently. Cite examples from each text to support your answer.
7. In what type of book would you be most likely to find each text?
8. Use a Venn diagram to compare and contrast the two texts. Use the following descriptors to get you started.
   •Informational Text or Literary Text •Prose or Poem •Emotional or Factual

Text 1 **Text 2**

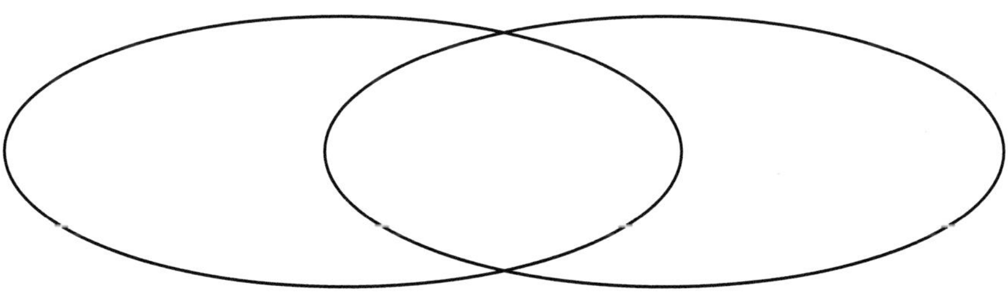

PART D: Write a poem that describes how rain affects you. Your poem can focus on practical or emotional effects. Be creative. Use descriptive language, and edit and proofread your work. Present your poem to your class.

U.S. Precipitation

Answer the questions as described in Parts A, B, and C.

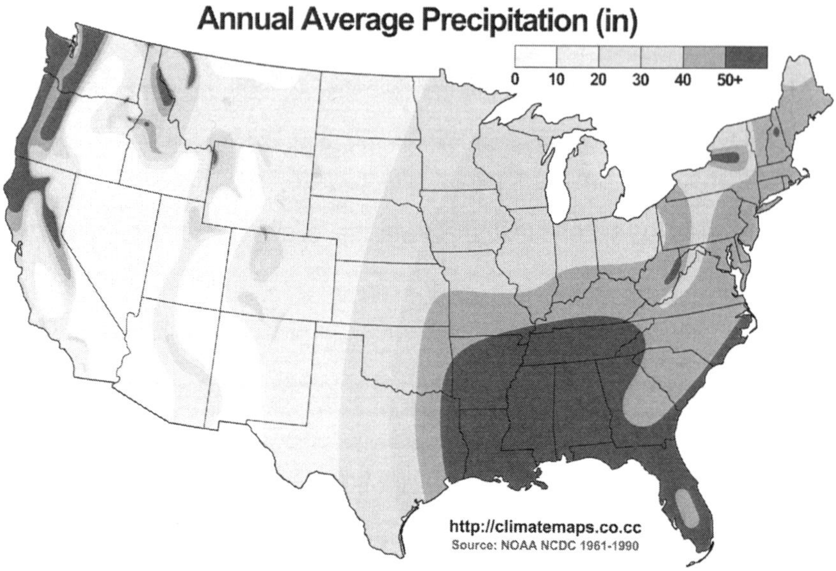

PART A: Look at the map and answer these questions.

1. A. What is the purpose of the map?
   B. What is the purpose of the map key?

2. A. Clearly explain in detail what data the map shows.
   B. Give an example of a possible way to use the data.

3. A. Which areas of the United States receive the most precipitation?
   B. Which areas of the United States receive the least precipitation?

4. Look at a map of the United States that shows geographic features.
   A. Make inferences about the influence of oceans on precipitation. Cite evidence from the maps to support your inferences.
   B. What natural features divide the areas with higher precipitation from the areas with lower precipitation? Make an inference about the effect these natural features have on precipitation.

WEATHER CENTER UPDATE

It looks like a rainy weekend ahead for most of the South, the East Coast all the way up to Pennsylvania, and parts of southern Vermont and New Hampshire. Expect a few heavy thunderstorms, and don't leave the house without an umbrella.

In the Midwest, a few light rains are expected, but not enough to keep the crops watered. Near-drought conditions have caused many crops to die, especially corn. Because many livestock, including pigs, cows, and chickens, are fed with corn, expect pork, cows, and chicken prices to rise in the coming months.

Western states are experiencing a severe drought. The lack of rainfall in the last year has caused a severe drought in Nevada, Utah, and parts of California. Temperatures are expected to remain high and the air will continue to be unusually dry for this time of year. No significant rainfall is expected in the Western states for another 5-7 days, a record-breaking dry spell. In southern California, the threat of wildfires remains high, as hot temperatures, lack of precipitation, and low levels of groundwater continue.

If you live near the coast in the Northwest, you can expect the usual—heavy rain.

PART B: Read the text and answer these questions.

5. What is the purpose of the text?
6. Use context clues to define drought as it is used in the text.
7. A. List at least two effects of drought in the Midwest.
   B. List at least two effects of drought in the Western states.
8. Explain the relationship between weather conditions and drought.

PART C: Compare and contrast the information in the map and text to answer this question.

9. Does the information in the map **support** or **contradict** the Weather Center Update? Cite three examples from both sources as evidence to support your answer.

Where in the World?

Look at the bar charts and answer the questions.

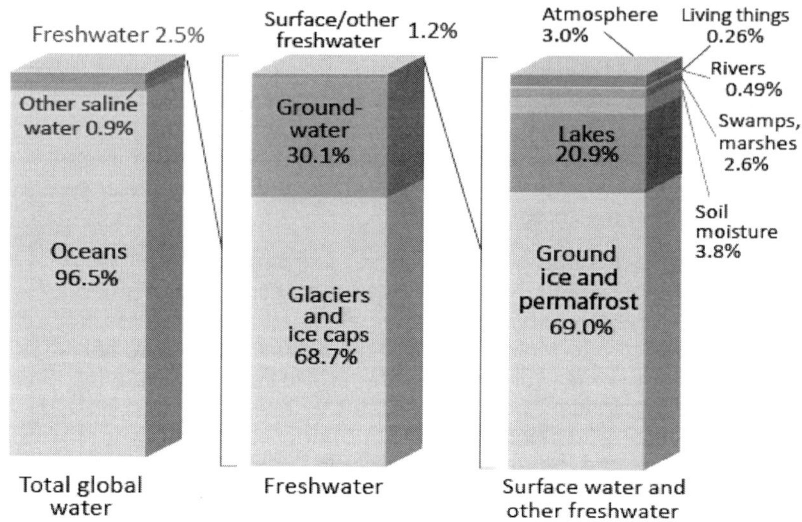

Graphic courtesy of United States Geological Survey

1. A. What is the purpose of the left bar chart?
   B. What is the purpose of the middle bar chart?
   C. What is the purpose of the right bar chart?
2. Explain the relationship between the left chart and the middle chart.
3. Explain the relationship between the middle chart and the right chart.
4. What is the purpose of the series/grouping of the three charts?
5. Analyze percentages in the chart to number the categories from largest (1) to smallest (6).
   A) _____Lakes
   B) _____Oceans
   C) _____All freshwater
   D) _____Glaciers and ice caps
   E) _____Atmosphere
   F) _____Surface/other freshwater
6. Use the data in the left bar chart to make a circle graph. Include a title, segments (approximately drawn is okay), segment labels, a key, and data source.

Water in Four Spheres

Read the text and complete Parts A, B, and C.

Water can be found in the hydrosphere, the cryosphere, the atmosphere, and the biosphere.

PART A: Choose one of the "spheres"—hydrosphere, cryosphere, atmosphere, or biosphere. Complete the KLW chart by writing what you already **know** about that "sphere" and at least five questions of what you **want** to learn. Then use at least two online resources to answer the questions you asked. Record your answers under "what I **learned**."

What I already **know:**	What I **want** to learn:	What I **learned:**
What I can **infer** by combining what I already knew with what I learned:		

PART B: Summarize what you learned into a short oral report. Tell what you learned and how your "sphere" relates to the water cycle. Proofread and edit your work.

PART C: Give your oral report to your class. Answer any questions about your topic.

Water Cycle Quotations

Jacques Cousteau was a famous scientist who studied the oceans.

Rewrite each quotation to complete the chart. Use the completed chart to answer the questions.

Jacques Cousteau quotations:	What each quote means to me:
"Water and air, two of the most essential fluids on which all life depends, have become global garbage cans."	
"We forget that the water cycle and the life cycle are one."	

1. What is the common theme between the two quotations?
2. Make at least 3 inferences about the author of the quotations. Support your inferences with evidence from the quotations.
3. Analyze each statement to determine whether the author would most likely **agree** or **disagree**.
   A. ____________ Fish, birds, and other forms of wildlife depend upon the water cycle in order to live.
   B. ____________ The pollution levels in the ocean have reached critical levels.
   C. ____________ What happens in the wild forests, oceans, and marshes has little impact upon human lives in towns and cities.
   D. ____________ Very few people live in the Sahara Desert in Africa, because rain rarely falls and no crops will grow.
   E. ____________ Approximately 60% of the human body is made of water. We must drink water to replace the water our bodies use.
   F. ____________ The ocean is so wide and so deep that throwing a little trash into the ocean cannot hurt anything.

PRIMARY SOURCE ANALYSIS

A River Runs Through It

Read the text, look at the photographs, and answer the questions.

The Colorado River is a major source of water for many cities in the western United States, including more than 30 million people in Los Angeles, Phoenix, Las Vegas, and Denver. However, water levels in the Colorado River are running low. People are using the river's water faster than it can be refilled with rainwater from precipitation and snowmelt from the Rocky Mountains. Lack of rain in the winter has caused water levels in the Colorado River to drop significantly. Warmer, drier summers have caused greater evaporation than normal. Higher temperatures have led to less snowfall in the Rocky Mountains, meaning less snowmelt flowing into the Colorado River. Low water levels in the Colorado River could be disastrous for the people in major Western cities.

1. Summarize the text by describing the 5 Ws:
   A. What is the problem?
   B. Where is it a problem?
   C. Why is it a problem?
   D. Who is it a problem for?
   E. When is it a problem?
2. How many months apart were the two photographs taken?
3. List at least 3-5 differences between the two photographs.
4. Use information from the text and photographs to list at least 5 reasons the water level of the Colorado River has changed.
5. Predict how low water levels in the Colorado River will affect animals, people, and crops in the West. Explain your response.

CAUSE & EFFECT

Polluted Water

Read the text and answer the questions.

> **VOCABULARY**
>
> **contaminated:** adj. exposed to harmful or poisonous substances

Water can become contaminated at any stage in the water cycle.

Air pollution contaminates water vapor in the atmosphere. Cars, trucks, and airplanes release harmful exhaust fumes into the air as they operate. Many businesses release chemicals into the air as a byproduct of their manufacturing process. Even the energy you use at home and school results in chemicals in the air. When poisonous chemicals combine with water in clouds, rain can turn into dangerous "acid rain."

Ground pollution contaminates water above and below ground. When it rains, chemicals and fertilizers used on farms and residential lawns washes into ponds and rivers or soaks into the ground. These chemicals poison plants and animals.

Ocean pollution contaminates water in the ocean. Oceans have become "dumping grounds" for trash like plastic bottles, metal cans, and old tires. Garbage from ships is commonly dumped in the ocean. Oil spills have had significant effects on the oceans. Additionally, rivers can bring land pollution to the ocean.

1. Use the text to complete the Graphic Organizer.

	Cause:		Effect:
Air pollution		→	
Ground pollution		→	
Ocean pollution		→	

2. Use logical reasoning to number the events in chronological order.

_____ Rain continuously washes lawn chemicals into a nearby stream.
_____ Bears begin to explore nearby towns, digging through trashcans and approaching people's homes looking for food.
_____ Over a five-year period, a lawn care business uses chemicals to kill weeds.
_____ Bears that usually eat fish from the stream cannot find enough food.
_____ Fish in the stream die from the high level of poisonous chemicals.
_____ Human-bear encounters and injuries increase.

Conservation Vocabulary

Read the text and answer the questions.

The water cycle is a <u>closed system</u>. That means no new water is added to the Earth and no existing water is removed. Water circulates, but the total amount does not change. Additionally, less than three percent of Earth's water is freshwater—what we need for drinking, bathing, watering plants, and most of our other uses.

Because there is no new water available, water is a <u>limited</u> natural resource. Freshwater is also a <u>scarce</u> resource, meaning there's not enough of a supply to meet everyone's demand. These factors make conservation of our water supply very important! If we waste or pollute our water, we won't have it available to use!

1. A. Use the text to define <u>closed system</u>.
   B. Describe what happens to water in a closed system.
2. Use the text to explain the difference between <u>limited</u> and <u>scarce</u>.
   A. Is salt water limited? B. Is salt water scarce?
   C. Is freshwater limited? D. Is freshwater scarce?
3. Use an online dictionary to write a short definition of each vocabulary word below. Then, classify each word as either a **PROBLEM** or **SOLUTION** for a healthy water cycle, and write it in the correct column in the table.

chemicals conservation drought environmentalism litter

overpopulation pollution recycling regulation wastefulness

PROBLEMS:	SOLUTIONS:

Correlations to Common Core State Standards

For your convenience, correlations are listed page-by-page, and for the entire book!

This book is correlated to the Common Core State Standards for English Language Arts grades 3-8, and to Common Core State Standards for Literacy in History, Science, & Technological Subjects grades 6-8.

Correlations are highlighted in gray. (Highlighted numbers are shown in bold below.)

PAGE #	READING *Includes:* RI: Reading Informational Text RST: Reading Science & Technical Subjects	WRITING *Includes:* W: Writing WHST: Writing History/Social Studies, Science, & Technical Subjects	LANGUAGE *Includes:* L: Language LF: Language Foundational Skills	SPEAKING & LISTENING *Includes:* SL: Speaking & Listening
2	RI RST · **1 2 3 4 5** 6 7 **8** 9 **10**	W WHST · 1 **2** 3 **4** 5 6 7 **8 9 10**	L LF · 1 2 3 **4 5 6**	SL · 1 2 3 4 5 6
3	RI RST · **1** 2 **3 4 5** 6 **7** 8 **9 10**	W WHST · 1 **2** 3 **4** 5 6 7 **8 9 10**	L LF · 1 2 3 **4 5 6**	SL · 1 2 3 4 5 6
4	RI RST · **1 2 3 4 5** 6 **7 8 9 10**	W WHST · 1 **2** 3 **4** 5 6 7 **8** 9 10	L LF · 1 2 3 **4** 5 **6**	SL · 1 2 3 4 5 6
5	RI RST · **1** 2 **3** 4 **5** 6 7 **8** 9 **10**	W WHST · 1 **2** 3 **4** 5 6 7 **8 9 10**	L LF · 1 2 3 4 5 6	SL · 1 2 3 4 5 6
6	RI RST · **1** 2 **3 4 5** 6 7 **8** 9 **10**	W WHST · **1 2 3 4** 5 6 7 **8 9 10**	L LF · 1 2 3 **4** 5 **6**	SL · 1 2 3 4 5 6
7	RI RST · **1 2 3** 4 **5 6** 7 **8** 9 **10**	W WHST · **1 2** 3 **4** 5 6 7 **8 9 10**	L LF · 1 2 **3 4** 5 **6**	SL · 1 2 3 4 5 6
8	RI RST · **1** 2 **3 4 5** 6 **7** 8 9 **10**	W WHST · 1 **2** 3 **4** 5 6 7 **8 9 10**	L LF · 1 2 3 **4** 5 **6**	SL · 1 2 3 4 5 6
9	RI RST · **1** 2 **3** 4 **5** 6 7 **8** 9 **10**	W WHST · 1 **2** 3 **4** 5 6 7 **8 9 10**	L LF · 1 2 3 **4** 5 **6**	SL · 1 2 3 4 5 6
10	RI RST · 1 **2 3 4 5** 6 **7 8** 9 **10**	W WHST · 1 **2** 3 4 5 6 7 8 **9 10**	L LF · 1 2 3 **4** 5 **6**	SL · 1 2 3 4 5 6
11	RI RST · **1 2 3** 4 **5 6 7** 8 **9 10**	W WHST · 1 2 3 4 5 6 7 8 9 10	L LF · 1 2 3 4 5 6	SL · 1 2 3 4 5 6
12-13	RI RST · 1 2 3 **4 5** 6 **7** 8 **9** 10	W WHST · 1 2 3 4 5 6 7 8 9 10	L LF · 1 2 3 4 5 6	SL · 1 2 3 4 5 6
14-15	RI RST · **1 2 3 4 5 6** 7 **8 9 10**	W WHST · **1 2 3 4 5** 6 7 **8 9 10**	L LF · 1 2 **3 4 5 6**	SL · **1 2** 3 **4** 5 **6**
16-17	RI RST · **1 2 3 4 5 6 7 8 9 10**	W WHST · 1 **2** 3 **4** 5 6 **7 8 9 10**	L LF · 1 2 3 **4** 5 **6**	SL · 1 2 3 4 5 6
18	RI RST · **1 2** 3 4 **5** 6 **7 8** 9 10	W WHST · 1 **2** 3 **4** 5 6 7 **8 9 10**	L LF · 1 2 3 4 5 6	SL · 1 2 3 4 5 6
19	RI RST · **1** 2 **3 4 5** 6 7 8 **9 10**	W WHST · 1 **2** 3 **4 5 6 7 8 9 10**	L LF · 1 2 3 **4** 5 **6**	SL · **1** 2 3 **4** 5 6
20	RI RST · **1 2 3 4 5 6** 7 **8 9 10**	W WHST · 1 **2** 3 4 5 6 7 8 **9 10**	L LF · 1 2 3 **4 5 6**	SL · 1 2 3 4 5 6
21	RI RST · **1 2 3** 4 **5** 6 **7 8 9 10**	W WHST · **1 2** 3 **4** 5 6 7 **8 9 10**	L LF · 1 2 3 4 5 6	SL · 1 2 3 4 5 6
22	RI RST · **1 2** 3 4 **5** 6 7 8 9 **10**	W WHST · 1 2 3 4 5 6 7 8 9 10	L LF · 1 2 3 **4** 5 **6**	SL · 1 2 3 4 5 6
23	RI RST · **1** 2 **3 4 5** 6 7 8 **9 10**	W WHST · 1 **2** 3 **4** 5 **6 7** 8 9 **10**	L LF · 1 2 3 **4 5 6**	SL · 1 2 3 4 5 6
COMPLETE BOOK	RI RST · **1 2 3 4 5 6 7 8 9 10**	W WHST · **1 2 3 4 5 6 7 8 9 10**	L LF · 1 2 **3 4 5 6**	SL · **1 2** 3 **4** 5 **6**

For the complete Common Core standard identifier, combine your grade + "." + letter code above + "." + number code above.

In addition to the correlations indicated here, the activities may be adapted or expanded to align to additional standards and to meet the diverse needs of your unique students!